williambee

williambee
Stanley's
Store

Published by
PEACHTREE PUBLISHERS
1700 Chattahoochee Avenue
Atlanta, Georgia 30318-2112
www.peachtree-online.com

First published in Great Britain in 2017 by Jonathan Cape,
an imprint of Random House Children's Publishers UK
First United States version published in 2017 by Peachtree Publishers

Illustrations rendered digitally.

Printed in December 2016 by Leo Paper in China
10 9 8 7 6 5 4 3 2 1
First Edition
ISBN 978-1-56145-868-4

Cataloging-in-publication data is available from the Library of Congress

williambee
Stanley's
Store

Ω
PEACHTREE
ATLANTA

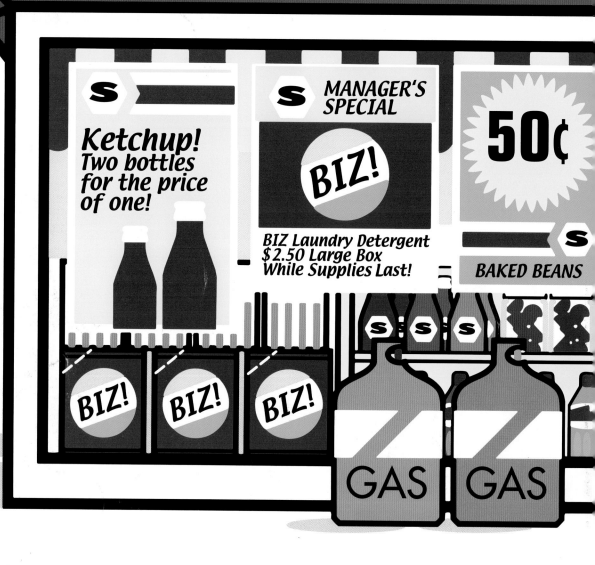

Ketchup!
Two bottles
for the price
of one!

MANAGER'S
SPECIAL

BIZ!

BIZ Laundry Detergent
$2.50 Large Box
While Supplies Last!

50¢

BAKED BEANS

BIZ! BIZ! BIZ!

GAS GAS

It's going to be another busy day at Stanley's Store.

Stanley is unloading fresh fruits
and vegetables from the truck.

His yellow forklift goes
PEEPPEEPPEEPPEEPEEP.

Hattie helps Myrtle pick out cheese.

Myrtle likes round cheese and square cheese and triangular cheese. In fact, she likes any shape of cheese!

Shamus and Little Woo are on their weekly shopping trip. Little Woo rides in the cart.

He is just the right height to reach
the sweets. Little Woo loves shopping.

Myrtle wants some nice bread
to go with her cheese.

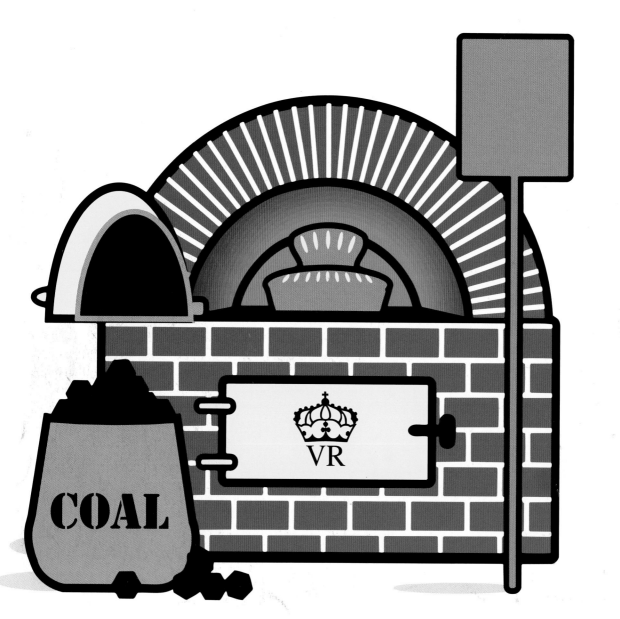

Gabriel gives her a cottage loaf
fresh from the oven.
Mind your fingers, Myrtle. It's still hot!

Stanley built a beautiful display
of fruits and vegetables.
Well done, Stanley!

Oh dear! Charlie isn't looking
where he's going...

. . .silly Charlie!

Red apples, green watermelons, purple plums, and lovely yellow bananas are everywhere!

At the cash register, Stanley rings up
Shamus and Little Woo's groceries.

What a lot of cookies and chocolates...

Myrtle bought too much cheese to carry.

How will she get it all home?

Luckily for Myrtle,
Stanley's Store delivers.

Thank you, Stanley! Thank you, Hattie!

Well! What a busy day!

Time for supper!
Time for a bath!

And time for bed!
Goodnight, Stanley.

Stanley

If you liked **Stanley's Store** then you'll
love these other books about Stanley:

Stanley the Builder   **Stanley's Garage**

Stanley's Diner   **Stanley the Mailman**

Stanley the Farmer

williambee